Penny, Snowman, and Chelsea's Adventure

Debra Knight

ISBN-13: 9798452209485

Cover design by: Art Painter

Library of Congress Control Number: 2018675309

Printed in the United States of America

The people in the images are models, and are

not related to the characters in the story.

This book is dedicated to my daughter Roshonda
who loves storytime.

Special thanks to my children Darrell,
Roshonda, and Javonda.

Darrell and Roshonda, thank you for your
support. Javonda, thank you for your dedicated
hours helping me with this project.

-Mom

Once Upon a Time, in a faraway land, where the clouds are always fluffy and white as snow, and the sand is soft and white. A land where the ocean flows back and forth in a beautiful crystal blue, and the humans and animals are all friends. Here you would find Penny flying back and forth over the ocean and watching as the humans sit on the beach with their families.

As Penny flies around, she spots a little girl sitting in the sand playing all alone. *I wonder why she is all by herself.* Penny thought. *I am going to go talk to her.* Penny made a smooth landing right in front of the little girl.

"Hi, my name is Penny. What's your name?" she asked.

"Hi, my name is Chelsea." replied the little girl.

"Chelsea, why are you all alone playing in the sand?" asked Penny.

Chelsea sighed, "My brother doesn't want to play with me, and my sister has her friends. So I have no one to play with."

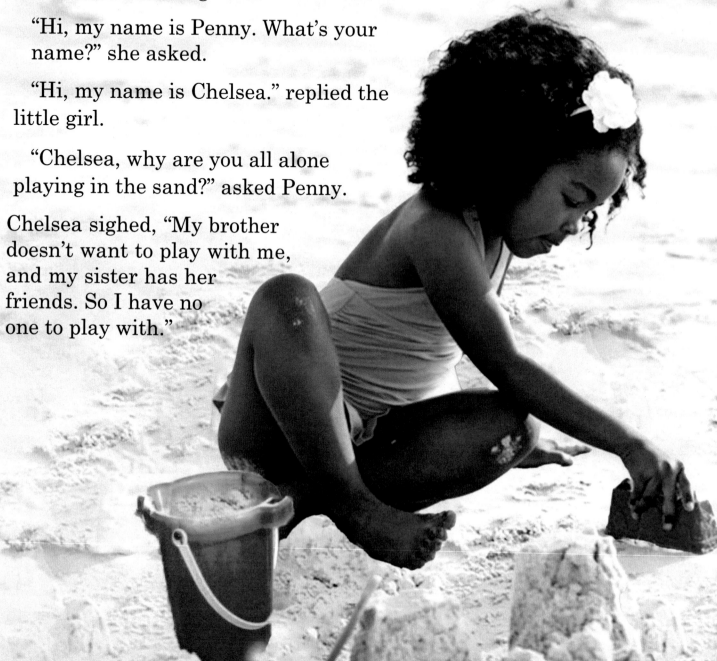

Penny looked around the beach; she noticed Chelsea's brother playing frisbee with a group of kids.

And her sister playing with her friends.

Aww, that's sad. Penny thought.

"Do you want to be my friend?" asked Penny.

Chelsea looked up quickly with big bright eyes,

"Oh yes, that would be nice!"

Penny had the perfect idea to make Chelsea's day brighter.

"Would you like to go for a ride?" she asked.

Chelsea whispered, "Yes!"

All Chelsea could see was this beautiful white unicorn.

Penny told Chelsea to jump on as she gave her special
glasses. Penny started slowly. They began to go higher and
higher into the beautiful blue sky.

"Wow, these glasses are so cool!"
Chelsea screamed with excitement, "I
can still see the ground even though
we are up so high!"

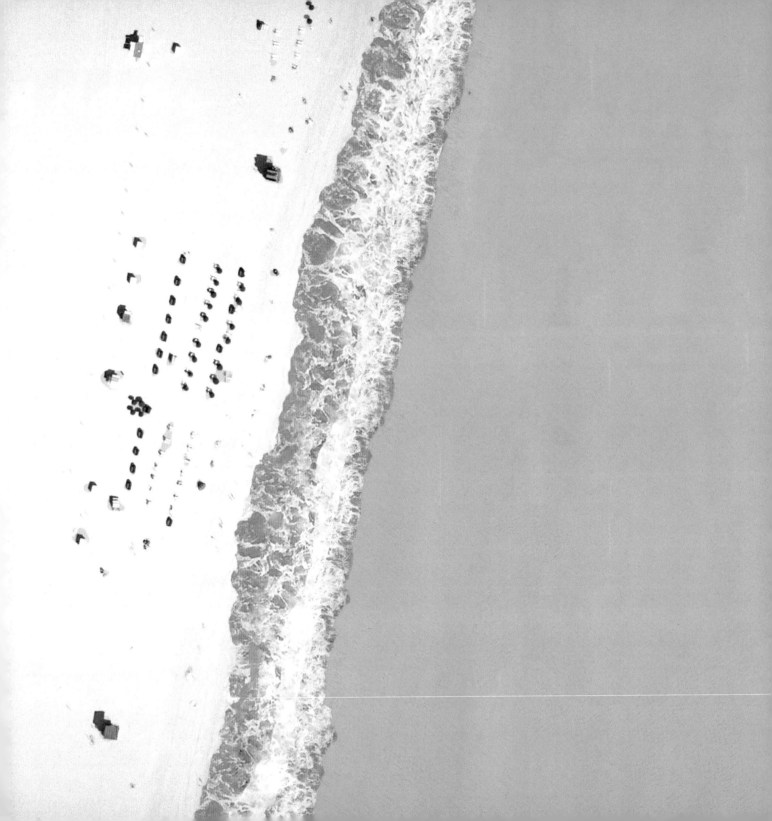

Chelsea was so excited when she saw the colorful rainbow stretched across the sky. It looked as if Penny was climbing up a staircase of colorful steps.

As they went higher and higher into the sky, it began raining
JJ Beans, Chelsea's favorite candy! She was even more excited;
she did not know what to do, so she just started to laugh.
Chelsea never had so much fun in her life!

As Penny flew away from the rainbow, it began to snow! Chelsea screamed, "Penny let's build a snowman!"

Penny flew around until she found the perfect spot filled with snow. She made a smooth landing, and they started to build a snowman.

As soon as Penny put the carrot nose on the snowman, he began to laugh!

"Let's name him Snowman!" shouted Chelsea as she hugged Snowman and started sliding through the snow.

Penny grinned as she watched Chelsea and Snowman.

Then she began gliding through the snow to follow them.

Round and down through the snow they went, laughing
and having so much fun.

Chelsea was having the time of her life, she
did not want it to end, but she knew she
would have to return home soon.

Chelsea thanked Snowman and hoped to see him again very soon. Snowman was delighted to have met Chelsea and hoped to see her again soon too!

Penny told Chelsea to jump on so she could take her back home.

As Chelsea and Penny flew back, they went lower and lower until they returned to the lovely faraway land. Where the clouds are always fluffy and white as snow, and the sand is soft and white. A land where the ocean flows back and forth in a beautiful crystal blue, and the humans and animals are all friends.

Penny went back to the place where she found Chelsea playing in the sand all alone. Penny made a smooth landing, and Chelsea climbed down.

Penny smiled and looked down at Chelsea, "Now that we are friends, you will never feel lonely, and you never have to play alone. Do not worry about your brother and sister not wanting to play with you. Now you have Snowman and me."

Penny's words warmed Chelsea's heart, and she smiled from ear to ear.

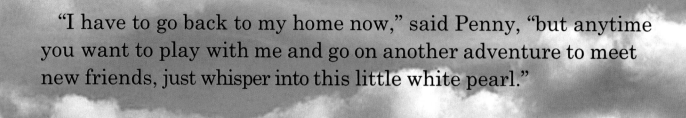

"I have to go back to my home now," said Penny, "but anytime you want to play with me and go on another adventure to meet new friends, just whisper into this little white pearl."

Penny gave Chelsea a beautiful purple necklace with one pearl stone and a charm shaped like a flower.

"See you later, my new friend. I had so much fun!" Penny said.

Chelsea thanked Penny and gave her a big hug.

Chelsea held her necklace tight in her hands and close to her heart as she watched Penny fly up into the sky, higher and higher until she disappeared.

Chelsea was so happy she wrote their names in the sand as she thought,

Penny, Snowman, and Chelsea, friends for life!